Iktomi
and the
Buffalo
Skull

Hi, folks!
I'M IKTOMI!
D'you like my mask?
Paul Goble says I've
got my head stuck
in a buffalo skull,
and can't see where I'm going!
It's just more white man's lies.
So don't let the children
hear about it. Huh?

Also by Paul Goble:

Iktomi and the Boulder
Iktomi and the Berries
Iktomi and the Ducks

Iktomi
and the
Buffalo
Skull

a Plains Indian story

told and illustrated
by PAUL GOBLE

Orchard Books   New York

for Janet and Robert, with all my love

References

Natalie Curtis, *The Indians' Book*, Harper and Brothers, New York, 1907. Ella C. Deloria, *Dakota Texts*, Publications of the American Ethnological Society, Vol. 14, New York, 1932. Frances Densmore, *Teton Sioux Music*, Bulletin 61, Bureau of American Ethnology, Washington, D.C., 1918. George Dorsey and Alfred Kroeber, *Traditions of the Arapaho*, Field Museum of Natural History, Anthropological Series, Vol. 5, Chicago, 1903. George Bird Grinnell, *By Cheyenne Campfires*, Yale University Press, New Haven, 1926. Alfred Kroeber, *Gros Ventre Myths and Tales*, Anthropological Papers of the American Museum of Natural History, Vol. 1, New York, 1908. Robert Lowie, *The Assiniboine*, Anthropological Papers of the American Museum of Natural History, Vol. 4, New York, 1910. Walter McClintock, *The Old West Trail*, Macmillan, London, 1910. Clark Wissler and D. C. Duvall, *Mythology of the Blackfoot Indians*, Anthropological Papers of the American Museum of Natural History, Vol. 2, New York, 1909.

Copyright © 1991 by Paul Goble. All rights reserved. No part of this book may be reproduced or transmitted in any form or by any means, electronic or mechanical, including photocopying, recording or by any information storage or retrieval system, without permission in writing from the Publisher. Orchard Books, A division of Franklin Watts, Inc., 387 Park Avenue South, New York, NY 10016. Manufactured in the United States of America. Printed by General Offset Company, Inc. Bound by Horowitz/Rae. The text of this book is set in 22 pt. Zapf Book Light. The illustrations are India ink and watercolor on Oram & Robinson (England) Limited Watercolour Board, reproduced in combined line and halftone. Library of Congress Cataloging-in-Publication Data. Goble, Paul. Iktomi and the buffalo skull : a Plains Indian story / told and illustrated by Paul Goble.   p.   cm. Includes bibliographical references. Summary: Iktomi, the Plains Indian trickster, interrupts a powwow of the Mouse People and gets his head stuck in a buffalo skull. Asides and questions printed in italics may be addressed by the storyteller to listeners, encouraging them to make their own remarks about the action. ISBN 0-531-05911-1   ISBN 0-531-08511-2 (lib.) 1. Indians of North America—Great Plains—Legends. 2. Tricksters—Great Plains—Juvenile literature. [1. Indians of North America—Great Plains—Legends.] I. Title. E78G73.G625 1990 398.2'08997078—dc20 [E]   90-7716 CIP AC 10 9 8 7 6 5 4 3 2 1   Book design by Paul Goble

About Iktomi

The story of the trickster who gets his head stuck in a skull was told throughout most of North America. Details vary as to how, or why, he got it stuck, and the skull changes from that of a bear in the versions from the Woodlands and Great Lakes, to an elk skull closer to the Rockies, or, on the Great Plains, the appropriate buffalo skull. The trickster is known by different names: Iktomi (*eek-toe-me*), which means "spider," is his Sioux name. He is also known as Old Man Coyote (Crow); Napi or Old Man (Blackfoot); Wihio or Ve'ho, which also means "spider" (Cheyenne). The trickster has the clever characteristics of "spider" and "coyote"; but he is a man, with the full range of human possibilities.

Sources for this story (see references) are among the oldest and most reliable, recorded by ethnologists and anthropologists during the first decade of this century. Indian people who had known the Buffalo Days were then old. Their grandchildren and great-grandchildren were being educated like white people, growing up without knowledge of or respect for the old ways. A wonderful cooperation arose between the scientists who wanted to record the mythology and ways of life accurately and the old people who wanted it all written down so future generations would never forget. Their records are printed in the museum and society publications of the time.

It needs to be mentioned that people of the Plains look upon a buffalo skull as sacred. Apart from temporary use as an altar in ceremonies, buffalo skulls were gathered up into spirit circles, the skulls facing inward, and left undisturbed with the elements. In this story Iktomi not only *sits* on one, he *peeks* inside....His irreverence brings retribution!

A Note for the Reader

Iktomi's thoughts, printed in small type, may break the flow of the story if they are read aloud. They can be mentioned when looking at the pictures.

The passages printed in gray italic give the reader the opportunity to encourage listeners to express their own thoughts about Iktomi's foolishness. It is customary for all present, young and old, to engage in considerable witticisms. Everyone has heard the story countless times, but the joy is in laughter and sharing it again. The story-teller, looking around with mock seriousness, and forefinger raised, waits for silence; and then takes up the story again....

Iktomi was walking along....
*Every story about Iktomi
starts the same way.*

I look good.

Yes, I'm looking good.

I'm looking very
good indeed.

My warbonnet

My fan

My silk shirt

My love-flute

My courting blanket

My trade-cloth leggings

My moccasins

Iktomi was walking along.
He was wearing all his best clothes.
He was going to get his horse.
"It's a great morning!"
he was thinking to himself.
"I'll ride over to the next village
and see my girlfriends."

We all know, don't we,
that Iktomi is already married?

I'm falling in love
with my playing.

"All the girls will be impressed
with my new clothes.
'Hey! Just look at Iktomi!' they'll say.
'Isn't he EXCITING! BREATHTAKING!!
I simply LOVE Iktomi!'
I'll pretend not to hear them,
and perhaps they'll say
more nice things about me."

*Iktomi always imagines that girls
think he is so terrific.*

"I'll play my love-flute.
All the girls will flock around me.
'Oh Ikto,' each will whisper to me,
'I can listen to you all day long.'"
Iktomi fingered his flute
and practiced some tunes.
His horse liked the sound,
and came walking up to him.

Indians aren't real
Indians nowadays.

I'm the last real
Indian.

I can kick too.

Iktomi told his horse:
"I want you to look good.
Today I'm going to be like
one of those real old-time chiefs,
sitting on your back.
Now, will you try to be a horse
worthy of a great chief?
Just this once? Will you?
Well, GET GOING!" he shouted,
and he kicked his horse
quite unnecessarily hard.

*Iktomi shouldn't be rude and unkind
to his horse, should he?*

How's that for a kick?

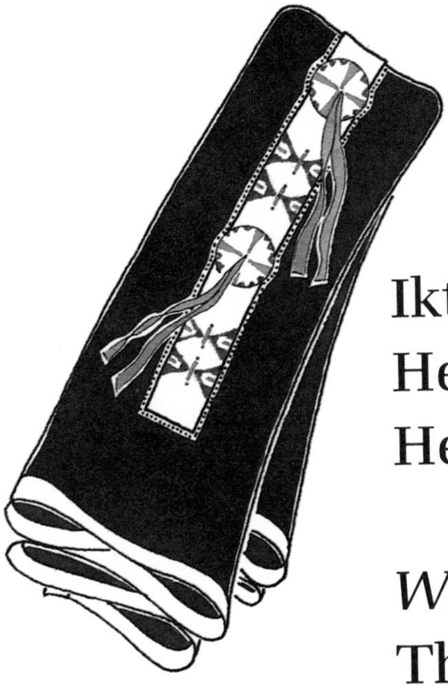

Iktomi rode on and on.
He was enjoying the ride.
He was feeling happy with himself.

WHOOOOOOOOOOOOOOSH!!!!
The horse bucked—
and Iktomi went flying—
and landed on his head.
"OUCH!"

Did anybody see that?

By the time Iktomi had picked
himself up,
his horse had galloped off
and was nowhere to be seen.

Am I dead?

I really prefer walking.
It's good exercise;
better for me.

Buffalo skull...
That's odd....
Yes, the white people
killed all the buffalo.

Iktomi was a long way from home,
and a long way from the next camp.
"Now what am I going to do?"
he wondered to himself.
"I'll have to walk back home.
I'll tell my wife I have been jogging."
Jogging in those clothes?

At that moment he heard singing....
He looked all around, but there was
nobody on the whole wide plain.
He could distinctly hear
high-pitched singing and drumming!
There was a dance going on
somewhere.
"Where is it?" he asked.

"It's a mystery," Iktomi said aloud.
"I can *hear* a powwow,
but I cannot *see* anybody."

His spirit stirred to the music.

The soles of his feet itched.
His moccasins began beating up
and down.
His eagle feathers moved and rustled,
and in a moment Iktomi was
dancing—
dancing to the beat of the mysterious
singing and drumming.

I'm a real traditional dancer.

When the song came to an end,
Iktomi sat down on a buffalo skull
to rest, and to think....

I don't usually make
those kinds of sounds.

Are there mice
inside my skull?

He jumped up with a fright!
The singing started again—
right underneath him!
It was coming from the buffalo skull.
He got down on his hands and knees
and peeked into an eye socket.
The Mouse People were having
a powwow inside the buffalo skull!

Iktomi thought the mice looked
so happy,
and their outfits so pretty.
"Oh...Little Brothers..." Iktomi said,
"you dance *so* gracefully.
Please let me join you."
"Oh no!" the mice replied.
"You are much too big.
You may put just your head inside.
But, whatever happens...don't sleep."

Iktomi had once taken lessons
from a medicine man,
so he knew a little magic—
just enough to make his head smaller,
and to squeeze it inside the skull.
The singing made Iktomi sleepy.
Soon he was fast asleep.
*Do you remember the mice told him
not to go to sleep?*
When the mice had finished dancing,
they nibbled off Iktomi's hair,
and carried it away to line their nests.

LULLABY

a wa wa   wa i-ni-na i-sti-ma-na a   a   wa wa

wa i-ni-na i-sti-ma-na a   a wa wa wa wa   i-

ni-na i-sti-ma-na a   a wa wa wa wa i-ni-na i-sti-ma-na a

ini'la ~ isti'mana   be still ~ sleep.

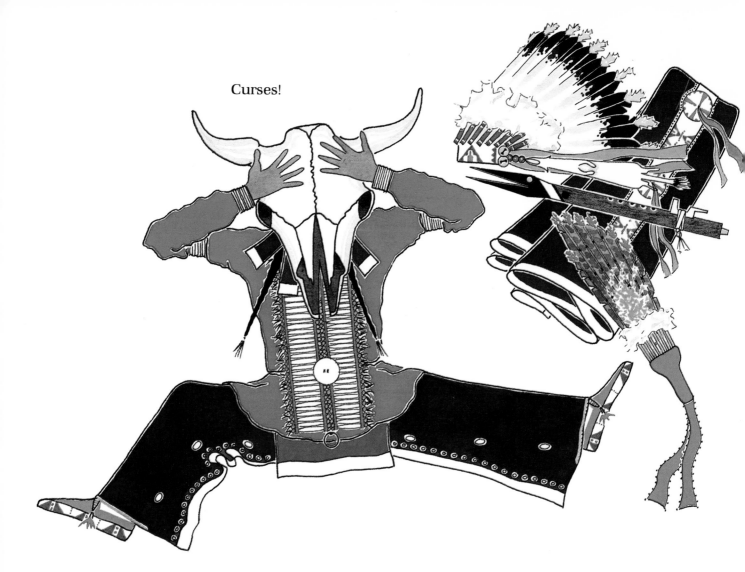

Curses!

When Iktomi awoke he found that
his head was stuck fast inside the skull.
He could not see anything.
All the magic he knew was
not enough to get the skull off again.
"If I can only find the river,"
he thought to himself,
"I can float down to my camp.
My wife will get this thing off me."

Iktomi had no idea where he was going.
He tripped and stumbled about blindly.
He got caught up in bushes,
and he fell into ravines.

Iktomi is really in trouble, isn't he?

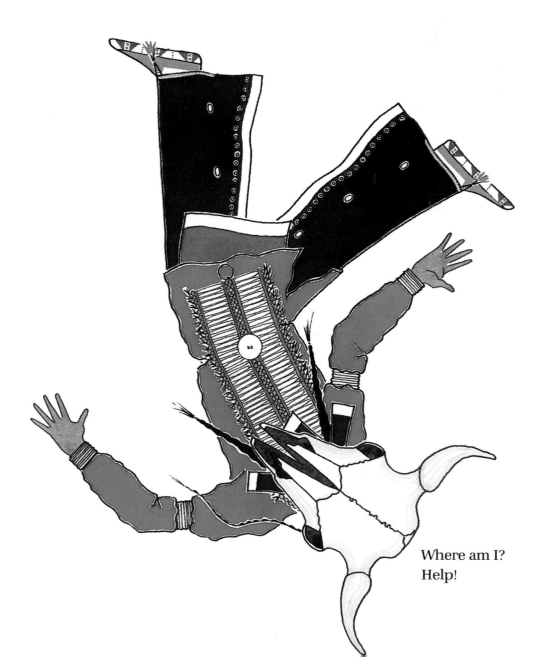

Where am I?
Help!

Iktomi crashed blindly into a tree.
"What kind of tree are you?"
he asked.
"I am Cottonwood," the tree replied.
"Ah! I must be close to the river,"
Iktomi said.
He bumped into another tree.
"Friend, what tree are you?" he asked.
"I am Willow," the tree answered.
"Then I must be right by the river,"
Iktomi said.
The next moment he stepped off
the bank—

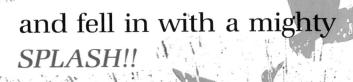

and fell in with a mighty
SPLASH!!

Iktomi floated down with the current.

The ducks laughed to see him:
"Hey! Look! It's Ikto! Hello, Ikto!
See! He's trying to make us laugh!
Hello, Buffalo Frog! You *do* look funny!
Won't Mrs. Iktomi have a good
laugh too!"

*He certainly wasn't meaning
to be funny, was he?*

This skull gives me
a terrible headache.

I thought I ate all
the ducks in the
last story....

When Iktomi heard voices,
he knew he had reached his camp,
and he called out in a hollow voice
from inside the buffalo skull:
"Help! It's me! Come and help! Quick!"

People ran away in terror.
"A talking skull!" they screamed.
"It's a spirit...a buffalo ghost!"
Nobody had any idea it was Iktomi.

Wouldn't that frighten you?

A few people were braver than the rest;
they threw their lariats over the horns,
and pulled Iktomi out of the water.
"Just look who we've got here!
It's Ikto!"
They laughed again and again.
"Hey! Your wife has been looking
for you all day long.
You better watch out!"

Careful, you louts!
My poor neck…

After being pulled by his neck
out of the river, Iktomi was half dead.
"Break this skull off my head,"
he gasped feebly.
His wife was angry.
She had her heavy stone hammer
which she used for breaking
marrowbones.
"You silly man," she scolded,
and gave him a WHACK on the skull,
which knocked him to his knees.
"You think I don't know where
you were going today?
To see girls! Indeed!
Do you think they wanted to see you?"
She BASHED the skull again,
and knocked Iktomi flat.
"Girls! At your age!
You, a married man!
I'll teach you to know better...."
and she knocked him down again—
CRACK!!
—and the skull fell off in pieces.

Without much hair,
and with an awfully sore head,
Iktomi went on his way again....
Who knows what he
will get up
to next....

Don't show the children
this picture.

Nobody loves me....
Let me think:
—People distract me—
WHAT was I about to do?

This story reminds us
not to put our noses
into other people's business,
and to remember that buffalo skulls
are sacred and must be respected.